A Note from the Author

Children are often kept in the dark when loved
ones are affected by cancer. However, they
understand more than we think. As a mother and
a physician, I wanted to write stories for children
to come to terms with different forms of cancer.

Dear Dhevnu
Thank you for coming
today, keep making
[illegible] friend. *[signature]*
2/16/19

This book is dedicated to the following individuals:

Regina Pomeranz Krummel, my valiant and inspiring mother-in-law, who is an educator, a published poet and author, and the inspiration for *Bubbe's Boo-boo*.

Beth Cooley Jordan, an unrelenting patron of many causes, including raising awareness for brain tumors, and my inspiration for *Aunty Beth Butterfly*.

My daughters, Amita, who the stories are based around, and Maya, who is too little to be part of these stories.

My wonderful husband, Daniel Pomeranz Krummel, and my parents, Samar and Kabita Sengupta, have all inspired me to be who I am today.

www.mascotbooks.com

Boo-boos and Butterflies

©2018 Soma Sengupta, M.D., Ph.D. All Rights Reserved. No part of this publication may be reproduced, stored in a retrieval system or transmitted in any form by any means electronic, mechanical, or photocopying, recording or otherwise without the permission of the author.

For more information, please contact:
Mascot Books
620 Herndon Parkway #320
Herndon, VA 20170
info@mascotbooks.com

Library of Congress Control Number: 2018900720

CPSIA Code: PBANG0416A
ISBN-13: 978-1-68401-745-4

Printed in the United States

Boo-boos and Butterflies

written by Soma Sengupta, M.D., Ph.D.
illustrated by Anna Krupa

Aunty Beth Butterfly

Aunty Beth is special. She loves flowers and butterflies, just like I do. She likes playing with butterfly stickers just like me.

Aunty Beth has a brain tumor with a long name that I do not know.

All I know is that I love my Aunty Beth and she makes me feel very loved.

We planted flowers together in the garden, and I like watering them with my watering can every day.

Even though Aunty Beth has long since passed to the land of sleep, I still see her in every flower and butterfly that comes my way.

Bubbe's
Boo-boo

My Bubbe, Rifka, is really cool. She has short hair with purple streaks, long dangly earrings, and hip clothes. My Bubbe also has a boo-boo.

Bubbe went to see the
doctor. She has something
called cancer.

I do not really understand what that is, except that it is a really bad boo-boo. I asked Bubbe if the boo-boo hurts, and she said that it just makes her feel tired.

Bubbe still plays in the sand with me and builds birthday cakes and sand castles.

We make the best beach buddies in the whole world!

Today Bubbe is going to have an operation for her cancer.

She told me that she is going to have her boo-boo cut out and that she will be better soon.

I am worried. I think that it will be an ouchie.

But my Bubbe is brave and strong, and she says that she will be better soon.

I hope that she will be well enough to play, sing, and dance with me.

Bubbe and I celebrate our birthday together. I want to celebrate my birthday with my Bubbe for many more years.

My dream is that my Bubbe's boo-boo never, ever comes back.

About the Author

Soma Sengupta, M.D., Ph.D., is a physician and a scientist. She received medical training and conducted doctoral research at Cambridge University in the U.K. She completed advanced medical and research training at Yale University, Johns Hopkins, and Harvard-affiliated hospitals. She specializes in taking care of patients with brain tumors. Outside of her professional life, Soma enjoys time with her two daughters Maya and Amita, husband Daniel, cat Riggoletto, and dog Peppa Puppy.